Louie's Goose

By **H.M. Ehrlich**

Illustrated by **Emily Bolam**

HOUGHTON MIFFLIN COMPANY BOSTON

Walter Lorraine Books

For Nathaniel Isaac

Walter Lorraine *wn* Books

Text copyright © 2000 by H. M. Ehrlich
Illustrations copyright © 2000 by Emily Bolam

www.houghtonmifflinbooks.com

Library of Congress Cataloging-in-Publication Data
Ehrlich, H. M.
    Louie's goose / by H. M. Ehrlich : Illustrated by Emily Bolam.
        p. cm.
    Summary: While spending the summer at the beach with his parents,
Louie has a wonderful time playing with his toy goose and even
rescues her from a big wave.
        ISBN 0-618-03023-9   PA ISBN 0-618-26008-0
        [1. Toys — Fiction. 2. Geese — Fiction. 3. Beaches — Fiction.]
I. Bolam, Emily, ill. II. Title.
P27.E3335Lo 2000   99-28566
[E] — dc21   CIP

Printed in the China for Harriet Ziefert, Inc.
HZI 10 9 8 7 6 5 4 3 2

Ever since Louie was a small baby, he spent
summer vacations at the beach with his
mother, his father, and Rosie, his goose.

Louie's goose went everywhere.
When he fished from the boat dock,
Rosie sat by his side.

When the tide was low, Louie took Rosie
to find clams and oysters in the sandy muck.

Rosie came along for French fries...

and ice cream.

Sometimes Rosie went up in the air;

sometimes Rosie stayed on the ground.Oops!

After awhile, Louie's goose began to wear out.

When her bill came loose, Louie cried,
"She's broken! But Mommy can fix her."

Louie watched and waited while his mother
put the yellow bill back on with snaps.

When white stuffing poked out from a hole in
Rosie's side, Louie begged, "Please, Mommy,
fix her again, so she won't be broken!"

Louie's mother put a patch on Rosie.

When Rosie lost one of her webbed feet,
Louie cried, "Now she's REALLY broken."

"She's only a little broken," said Louie's father.
"I'll sew the foot back on with strong thread."

One sunny morning when they were on
the beach, Louie left Rosie near the shore
and went off to make a sandcastle.

A big wave picked up Rosie and
tossed her around in the ocean.

Then another wave carried Rosie to shore
and left her all wet and soggy on the sand.

Louie carried Rosie to his mother.
He cried, "Fix Rosie. Fix her! Fix her!"

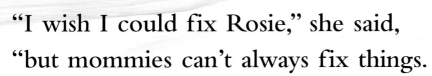

"I wish I could fix Rosie," she said,
"but mommies can't always fix things.
Maybe you can help her."

Louie hugged Rosie and sang to her:

Hush-a-bye, I'll make you cozy.
Go to sleep, my little Rosie.

He whispered, "I'm sorry you're cold and wet.
You need to rest. I'll be back soon."

Later, after Louie decided Rosie had been
resting long enough, he picked her up
and checked her all over.

Then he rushed up the beach
toward his mother.

"Mommy, Daddy!" he shouted.
"Guess what? Rosie is almost dry.
The sun fixed her!"

"Cozy, Rosie?" asked Louie.
And he gave his goose a hug.